THE DOG
WHO WANTED
TO FLY

THE DOG WHO WANTED TO FLY

by Kathy Stinson • art by Brandon James Scott

annick press
toronto + berkeley

Designed by Alexandra Niit

Annick Press Ltd.

We acknowledge the support of the Canada Council for the Arts and the Ontario Arts Council, and the participation of the Government of Canada/la participation du gouvernement du Canada for our publishing activities.

Funded by the Government of Canada · Financé par le gouvernement du Canada

Canada

ONTARIO ARTS COUNCIL
CONSEIL DES ARTS DE L'ONTARIO
an Ontario government agency
un organisme du gouvernement de l'Ontario

Cataloging in Publication

Stinson, Kathy, author

   The dog who wanted to fly / by Kathy Stinson ; art by Brandon James Scott.

Issued in print and electronic formats.

ISBN 978-1-77321-280-7 (hardcover).–ISBN 978-1-77321-282-1 (HTML).–

ISBN 978-1-77321-281-4 (PDF)

   I. Scott, Brandon, 1982-, illustrator II. Title.

PS8587.T56D64 2019   jC813'.54   C2018-905056-X

                                                C2018-905057-8

Published in the U.S.A. by Annick Press (U.S.) Ltd.
Distributed in Canada by University of Toronto Press.
Distributed in the U.S.A. by Publishers Group West.

Printed in China

www.annickpress.com
www.kathystinson.com
www.brandonjamesscott.com

Also available as an e-book.
Please visit www.annickpress.com/ebooks.html for more details.

To Georgia
—K.S.

For Perley James. Never stop wanting to fly.
—B.J.S.

Zora stared at a squirrel chittering on the fence.

When the squirrel ran, Zora ran too.
Not fast enough. She was *never* fast enough.
Chitterchitterchitterchitterchitter!
"If only I could fly," Zora said.
"*Then* I could catch that squirrel!"

CHITTER!
CHITTER!
CHITTER!
CHITTER!
CHITTER!

Tully said, "Dogs can't fly."

"I bet *I* can," said Zora. "Watch me!"
Zora bounced on the pads of her feet,
her nose high in the air.

CRASH!

She flapped her ears and wagged her tail.

SPLASH!

Up went kids on a teeter-totter. Maybe from up there . . .

When the kids got off, Zora raced on.

THUNK!

Zora said, "Flying is harder than it looks."
"That," said Tully, "is because *dogs can't fly.*"
Chitterchitterchitter!
Zora had to fly—to catch that squirrel
and to prove Tully wrong!

Across the sky floated a kite.

Zora grabbed a picnic umbrella.
She dashed up a hill, and—

"Drop it! Drop it!"
Zora, a good dog, dropped the umbrella.

Above her flew a giant airplane.
Surely if someone as big as a plane could fly . . .

Zora lay on her stomach,
her legs stretched out.
She whispered,
"Up!
Up!
Up!!"

Above her flew a giant airplane.
Surely if someone as big as a plane could fly . . .

Zora lay on her stomach,
her legs stretched out.
She whispered,
"Up!
Up!
Up!!"

Zora sighed.
She could jump up.
She could shake a paw.
She could roll over and take a bow.
Why couldn't she fly?
Chitterchitterchitter!
Chitterchitterchitter!
Tully was right.
She would never catch that squirrel.
Toward her doghouse she trudged.
Just then—

"Help! Help!"
Tully was in danger!

Zora's everything tingled!
All at once her tail pointed
straight out behind her,
her ears peeled back against
her head, the pads of her
feet became *jet* pads and—

Zora flew!
Zora soared!
Her everything *zzzzinged!*

"Got you, Tully!"

Tully said, "Not bad . . . for a dog."

And the squirrel was very quiet.